51461

Antioch Community High School
Library
1133 S. Main Street
Antioch, IL 60002

DEMCO

TEENS IN ENGLAND

Teens in

England

by Elizabeth Willingham

Content Adviser: Mark Bevir, Ph.D.,
Acting Director of the Center for British Studies,
University of California, Berkeley

Reading Adviser: Katie Van Sluys, Ph.D.,
Department of Teacher Education,
DePaul University

Compass Point Books ✦ Minneapolis, Minnesota

Compass Point Books
3109 West 50th Street, #115
Minneapolis, MN 55410

Editor: Julie Gassman
Designers: The Design Lab and Jaime Martens
Photo Researcher: Eric Gohl
Cartographer: XNR Productions, Inc.
Library Consultant: Kathleen Baxter

Art Director: Jaime Martens
Creative Director: Keith Griffin
Editorial Director: Nick Healy
Managing Editor: Catherine Neitge

Library of Congress Cataloging-in-Publication Data
Willingham, Elizabeth.
Teens in England / by Elizabeth Willingham.
   p. cm. — (Global connections)
ISBN-13: 978-0-7565-2061-8 (library binding)
ISBN-10: 0-7565-2061-4 (library binding)
1. Teenagers—England. 2. Teenagers—England—Social life and customs. I. Title. II. Series.

HQ799.G72E576 2007
305.2350942—dc22   2007006225

Visit Compass Point Books on the Internet at www.compasspointbooks.com
or e-mail your request to custserv@compasspointbooks.com

Table of Contents

ATLANTIC
OCEAN

ICELAND

NORWAY
SWEDI

SCOTLAND

NORTHERN
IRELAND

UNITED
KINGDOM

DENMARK

IRELAND

ENGLAND

NETHS

GERMANY

WALES

BELGIUM

LUX.

CZECH

FRANCE

AUSTRI

SWITZERLAND

SLOVEN

PORTUGAL

ANDORRA

ITALY

SPAIN

MOROCCO

TUNISIA

ALGERIA

NIGER

BRAZIL

London ⭐

BURKINA
FASO

ST

BENIN

TOGO

GHANA

NIGERIA

CAMEROON

EQUATORIAL GUINEA

SAO TOME & PRINCIPE

GABON

CO

RUSSIA

KAZAKHSTAN

CHINA

KYRGYZSTAN

UZBEKISTAN

TAJIKISTAN

NEPAL

INE

OVA

TURKMENISTAN

GEORGIA

AZERBAIJAN

ARMENIA

AFGHANISTAN

TURKEY

IRAQ

IRAN

PAKISTAN

CYPRUS

SYRIA

LEBANON

OMAN

KUWAIT

ISRAEL

JORDAN

QATAR

OMAN

U.A.E.

EGYPT

SAUDI ARABIA

INDIAN OCEAN

MALDIVES

YEMEN

ERITREA

SUDAN

ETHIO

C

UGANDA

KENYA

PUBLIC

RWANDA

O

BURUNDI

TANZANIA

MALAWI MOZAMBIQUE MADAGASCAR

SOME ENGLISH TEENS ARE GROWING UP IN THE CITY, others on a farm. Some attend state schools, others independent boarding schools. No matter what their background, teens are shaping not only their own lives but also the world around them.

English teens depend on each other for advice, support, and, of course, fun. Time with mates is time well-spent. Whether playing a game of cricket, shopping in a city center, or just hanging out at home, teens can always entertain themselves and each other.

Approximately 21 percent of England's population is between the ages of 11 and 19. By age 16 or 17, about half of teens are working full time. Others continue to attend school in preparation for university study. Teens who join the military take part in national defense, overseas peace missions, and emergency services. As adults, these teens will offer vital services to the next generation.

Exams and uniforms are two key features of England's education system.

CHAPTER ONE

Deciding Their Future

FROM THE TIME CHILDREN ARE YOUNG, FAMILIES IN ENGLAND HAVE TO MAKE A NUMBER OF IMPORTANT DECISIONS REGARDING SCHOOL. They must decide between a government-sponsored school and one that charges tuition. And within those two categories, there are a number of options. Goals, admission procedures, and coursework vary from school to school. Parents and students learn about individual schools to find the best fit.

The decisions continue through the years. By age 14, students make choices that will directly affect their future. They begin choosing courses with careers in mind. They may start on an academic path that includes continuing on to university. Or they may plan to spend fewer years in school and get a more general or vocational education.

From ages 5 to 16, all children in England are entitled to a free education at a state school. State schools receive funding from the national government and may be maintained by government officials. Most state schools are co-ed, with boys and girls

Lab work gives students an opportunity for hands-on learning in science courses.

attending classes together.

The majority of state-schools are mainstream schools. That means they provide a general education based on the national curriculum. As a result, all state school students study the same subjects. The government has required, for instance, that all 15-year-olds take courses in English, "maths" (mathematics), and science. They also study information technology, physical education, and citizenship.

Almost all schools require students to study French. They also receive sex education and career education. Schools must also provide religious education for their pupils. However, parents can withdraw their children from these courses.

Understanding the System

England's education system is organized into blocks of years called key stages. There are four key stages, which cover

Other Options

In addition to mainstream schools, students may opt for any of a number of other state schools that vary in focus. They include:

Special schools

These serve children with special educational needs, such as those with physical disabilities or learning difficulties.

Specialist schools

Here the focus is on a particular subject area—such as sports, technology, or the arts—while providing a broad education.

City technology colleges

Found in urban areas, these schools focus on science, technology, and vocational careers.

Faith schools

Emphasis is placed on religious studies in addition to the national curriculum.

Grammar schools

These are highly focused on traditional academics.

11 years of school. The majority of young English children enter primary school at age 4 or 5.

At the end of each key stage, students take a national exam to assess their progress. At the end of key stage 3, for example, students take a seven- to eight-hour test on English, maths, and science.

Teachers also evaluate each child's

The Key Stages

Ages	Stage
5–7	Key Stage 1
7–11	Key Stage 2
11–14	Key Stage 3
14–16	Key Stage 4

Paying for School

About 10 percent of English children attend one of the country's 2,300 independent schools. These schools are funded mainly by tuition fees paid by the students. The schools set their own curriculum

classroom work. This helps students and their parents get a well-rounded view of their progress. A key stage 3 teacher classroom assessment covers a number of courses. Topics range from English and maths to geography and physical education.

At the end of key stage 4, students have an important decision to make. They can choose to leave school and get a job. Or they can choose to stay in school for two more years in preparation for higher education. The students' test scores and individual interests are major factors in making these decisions. Also, teachers often encourage students toward specific career paths. Perhaps a teacher notices that a student is very good at mathematics or woodworking. The instructor may recommend a specific university or a technical school.

Independent schools tend to have lower student-to-teacher ratios than state schools. As a result, students may receive more personalized attention.

and admission requirements. However, the Department for Education and Skills monitors each independent school. The government officials want to ensure that the school maintains national standards.

Many English independent schools have excellent academic reputations.

To have a son at Eton or a daughter at Benenden, for instance, is a mark of high ambition and privilege. Most independent schools accept only boys or only girls. But many boys schools, such as Rugby, accept girls in the last two years of school.

All About Eton

One of England's most well known independent schools is Eton College in Berkshire. King Henry VI founded the school in 1440. Today nearly 1,300 boys ages 13 to 18 attend the respected school.

All of the students are required to live in the school's houses. School leaders believe that "boarding requires a boy to take responsibility for his own life and to get on with a community of other people." Each house holds about 50 boys and is supervised by a housemaster.

Prince William, second heir to England's throne, and his brother, Prince Harry, both attended Eton. Members of royal families from Africa and Asia have also attended. Even fictional characters such as Captain Hook and James Bond are said to be alumni of the school.

Eton students are surrounded by the historic architecture of their campus.

The majority of students at these schools live in dormitories on the grounds for the full school year. They return home only for holidays, or vacations. Some of these schools also accept "day girls" and "day boys." These students attend boarding school but live at home.

The cost of independent schools is extremely high for most families.

The average yearly fee for a boarding school in 2006 was 18,828 pounds (U.S.$37,103). Scholarships are available to needy families, but they usually cover no more than half of the costs.

Dressed for Success

Each day, students must wear a clean set of clothes that meet the dress code or uniform list standards. Students and

Uniforms are worn by students of all ages.

their families are responsible for buying school uniforms. Before the start of each term, shop windows in towns and cities are full of mannequins dressed in blazers or pleated skirts. Uniforms can be quite expensive, but many schools offer secondhand uniforms at the school store. If the cost of school clothes is too much for a family, schools or the government sometimes provide funds to help buy uniforms.

Uniforms are required at almost all English schools, whether independent or state-run. For girls, most uniforms consist of a white shirt, a V-necked jumper (sweater) with the school's logo, a school tie, black shoes, and long pants or a pleated skirt with stockings. Boys' uniforms are similar, with gray or black trousers instead of a skirt. In the summer, shorts are permitted, and girls also may wear summer dresses.

The color of the girls' jumpers is selected by the school, and many have stitching details in the school color. Schools often require blazers with the school patch on the sleeve or breast. Also, students must have different uniforms for outdoor wear. They often need gym clothes for outdoor sports, a scarf in school colors, or a certain type of coat.

All school uniforms are essentially alike. It can be difficult for students to show their individual personalities through their clothing. Not surprisingly, personal statements are sometimes made through accessories. Where

Some schools' dress codes specify appropriate hair length and styles.

allowed, different hairstyles, makeup, and jewelry can help a student stand out from the crowd.

A student's school uniform can play a part in his or her future. The "school colors" of boarding schools identify alumni to one another. Those wearing their school colors will be welcomed into alumni clubs. In addition, graduates of certain schools often feel obliged to help each other. The "old school tie" can give people advantages in politics and business.

School Schedules

Both state and independent schools follow similar calendars. The school year starts in early September and runs until early July. Boarding students may leave home a few days early to get settled into their dormitories.

Most schools give students two weeks off at Christmas, two weeks off at Easter, and six weeks off for the summer. Shorter breaks for local holiday celebrations may also be granted. Taking advantage of these school schedules, many families vacation together while the children are out of school.

Classes at a typical state primary school begin around 9 A.M. Students have three or four subjects before lunch. Most schools allow 45 minutes to go through the lunch queue (line), find a seat, and eat before returning to classes. Because of this time crunch, many students prefer to bring lunch from home. A packed lunch gives them more

control over what they eat. And it saves the expense of buying their lunch—typically around 1.50 pounds (U.S.$3). Bringing food from home also gives students more time to sit and talk with their friends.

After lunch and recess, classes continue for another few hours. When school is over, many kids go to an after-school activity, such as chess club or football (soccer) club. After dinner, most students start on homework. Students in college-preparatory courses can have up to an hour's worth of math problems and reading to do before bedtime.

In an independent school, the average day is similar to that in a state school. For boarding students, though, there is no need to worry about transportation or packing a lunch. Students usually get ready for the day and go to a common room to eat breakfast between 6 and 7:30 A.M. Like state schools, most boarding schools have classes from around 9 A.M. until 3:30 P.M. There are five 40-minute classes in the morning. After the first three, there is a break for students to return to their rooms for "elevenses." This midmorning tea often provides students with a snack. Two more classes follow, and then students have dinner, which is the midday meal.

What's for Lunch?

Many school lunches start with soup and bread. This course is followed by a main dish such as lamb curry, roasted chicken, or a vegetarian option. Sides of baked potatoes and salad bars are offered, as are traditional fast foods such as pizza and sausage rolls. Milk, milk shakes, juices, and bottled water are available at most schools. In addition, most schools offer daily desserts—commonly custards, fruits, yogurts, and tarts.

Whatever is served, schools aim to meet the nutritional standards set by the United Kingdom (UK) government. Meals are balanced, with starches; dairy food; meat, fish, and other proteins; and at least two daily portions of vegetables and fruits. Fried foods are limited to two per week, and candy, potato chips, and soft drinks are banned.

A Look at Electives

Perhaps the biggest difference between state schools and independent schools is the type of electives and activities offered. Young people who attend an independent school such as Harrow or Clifton are able to pick from many sports and activities. Most state schools cannot afford to offer the same range. Here are some of the choices:

Sports at Harrow School	Activities at Clifton College
Archery	Athletics Fitness Training
Badminton	Backgammon/Chess Club
Basketball	Ceramics
Cricket	Chemistry Club
Croquet	Cooking
Cross-country	Creative Writing
Football (soccer)	Dance
Gymnastics	Debate Club
Hockey	Diving
Judo	Fencing
Polo	Forensics (criminal)
Riding	Photography
Rock climbing	Space/Astronomy Society
Rowing	String Orchestra
Rugby	Swing Band
Sailing	Textiles
Shooting	Trampolining
Squash	Wind Band
Swimming	Yoga

After dinner, students take more classes or participate in sports or arts and crafts, depending on their personal preference. A lucky student may return to the dormitory to find a care package from his or her gran (grandmother). It is polite to share the package of small gifts and treats with one's roommates. In the evening, supper is eaten as a group. Lights go out around 8:30 or 9 P.M.

Special School Days

Even with a challenging academic schedule, some school days in England are dedicated to fun social activities. Choirs and bands give public performances. Sporting events, especially football games, are always well-attended. School dances are highly popular events as well. Since some state schools are still single-sex, a boys school may pair up with a nearby girls school to hold a dance.

Still other school activities are religious. Most English schools are connected in one way or another with the Church of England, so all major Christian holidays are days off for students. A festive yearly tradition for Christians—Christmas pageants—are common in most English schools. Pupils of other religions can take days off for their own holidays without affecting their attendance records.

Other important school events are

School plays are common in both state and independent schools.

GCSE exams for certain subjects can be quite long and stressful for some students.

test days. There are two major academic tests. One is the test for the General Certificate of Secondary Education (GCSE), which students take at age 15 or 16. The GCSE exam covers the basics and is a big factor in deciding whether to stay in school for another two years. Students who do not do well on the test may choose to leave school and enter the workforce. In contrast, students who earn high marks are encouraged to stay in school and prepare for college.

At the end of the extra two years of school, students take the other major academic test, the A-Level exams in three subjects. These are considered college-entrance exams. The results determine admission into universities. Those with the highest scores earn spots in the best universities.

There are also National Vocational Qualifications (NVQ) exams. These tests help determine whether a student who is in a nonacademic career track has attained the best education possible. NVQs are administered in areas such as catering, tourism, business and management studies, social services, construction, engineering, and plant and animal care.

Though graduation seems far off to students just entering school, the big day eventually does come. About 30 percent of students go on to study at universities. Others decide to enter the workforce. Very little fuss—such as graduation ceremonies or yearbook signings—is made over finishing studies at boarding and state-run schools. Students begin school as children and leave at age 16 or 18—well on their way to a career.

Teen Scenes

In London, a 14-year-old girl climbs the stairs leading out of the Tube (subway) station on her way to school. Today she will take the national tests that all key stage 3 students must take. The exams will help her decide what sort of courses she should take next year in school. Even though graduation won't come for at least two years, she needs to choose subjects that will give her the best options for her future job.

About three hours away, a 16-year-old boy rides the bus to school in the Devon countryside. His thoughts are also on test-taking. His exams for his General Certificate of Secondary Education are coming up. When his required education is completed, he'll join his father full time on the family dairy farm.

In Manchester, a 17-year-old girl hurries to work at a local hair salon. She started out washing hair and sweeping up, but soon decided she would like to be trained as a hairdresser. She is considering going to a vocational program to learn the trade, but is hoping that the salon owner will offer her an apprenticeship.

Teens in England begin thinking about careers at a young age. Whether they leave school at age 16 or continue on to A-Level studies, young people have many options to prepare for future careers.

Walking and biking are among the most common ways for teens to get around busy English cities.

2

From City Flats to Country Cottages

MANY TEENS THROUGH-OUT ENGLAND—AND THE WORLD, FOR THAT MATTER—share interests and pastimes. However, a teen's typical day varies widely. There are a number of influences that affect daily life. The type of school teens attend, income and background, and of course, the individual families all have a part in shaping day-to-day activities.

One of the strongest influences on daily life is where people live. How teens get to school, what type of home they live in, and after-school activities all depend on whether their home is in a bustling city or a green countryside.

The majority of the population in England is urban. According to the 2001 UK census, eight out of 10 citizens lived in urban areas. London is the most populated by far. It boasts a density of 11,815 people per square mile (4,726 per square kilometer). In comparison, the North West region has the second highest density, with 1,210 people per square mile (484 per sq km).

England & the UK

The United Kingdom of Great Britain and Northern Ireland is one political entity. It comprises the countries of England, Scotland, Wales, and Northern Ireland. This group of countries operates together under one government. It can be loosely compared to the United States, where there are many independently governed states that follow one federal government. In the United Kingdom, each country has its own legal system and way of life. But all of these countries obey one central government in matters of political unity and general law.

England is also part of Great Britain (also known simply as Britain). This island is divided into England, Scotland, and Wales. Across the Irish Sea is a second island. The Republic of Ireland (Éire), a country that is not part of the United Kingdom, takes up most of the island. Northern Ireland, which makes up the remainder, is part of the United Kingdom.

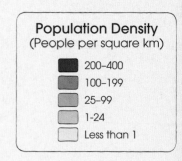

Population Density
(People per square km)

- 200–400
- 100–199
- 25–99
- 1–24
- Less than 1

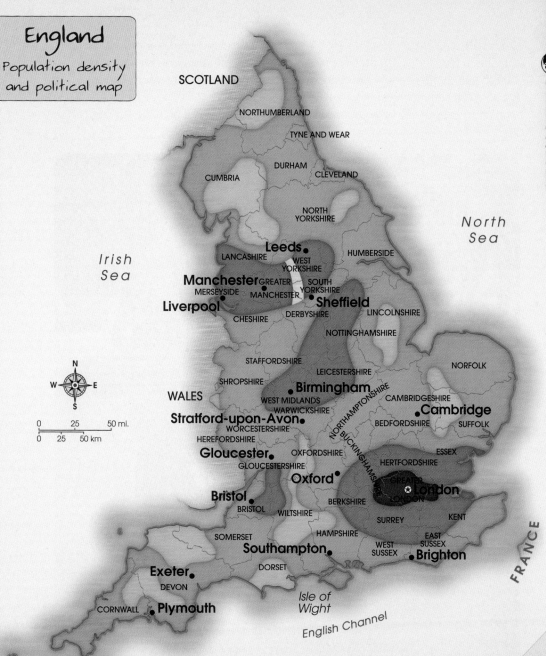

England
Population density and political map

SCOTLAND

NORTHUMBERLAND

TYNE AND WEAR

CUMBRIA

DURHAM

CLEVELAND

NORTH YORKSHIRE

North Sea

Irish Sea

LANCASHIRE

Leeds

WEST YORKSHIRE

HUMBERSIDE

Manchester GREATER MANCHESTER

MERSEYSIDE

SOUTH YORKSHIRE

Liverpool

CHESHIRE

DERBYSHIRE

Sheffield

LINCOLNSHIRE

NOTTINGHAMSHIRE

STAFFORDSHIRE

LEICESTERSHIRE

NORFOLK

SHROPSHIRE

Birmingham

WALES

WEST MIDLANDS

WARWICKSHIRE

NORTHAMPTONSHIRE

CAMBRIDGESHIRE

Cambridge

Stratford-upon-Avon

WORCESTERSHIRE

BEDFORDSHIRE

SUFFOLK

HEREFORDSHIRE

Gloucester

OXFORDSHIRE

BUCKINGHAMSHIRE

ESSEX

GLOUCESTERSHIRE

HERTFORDSHIRE

Oxford

GREATER LONDON

London

Bristol

BRISTOL

BERKSHIRE

KENT

WILTSHIRE

SURREY

SOMERSET

HAMPSHIRE

WEST SUSSEX

EAST SUSSEX

Southampton

Brighton

DORSET

Exeter

DEVON

Isle of Wight

CORNWALL

Plymouth

English Channel

FRANCE

Isles of Scilly

ATLANTIC OCEAN

N
W E
S

0   25   50 mi.
0   25   50 km

The Day-to-Day

City life in England is usually very fast-paced. Teens who live in cities tend to become self-sufficient, especially those who take buses or subways to school.

On a typical weekday morning, before heading off to school, teenagers eat a breakfast of cold cereal or toast and jam and tea.

After-school activities in English

Groups of teens are a common sight in city shopping districts.

cities vary widely. In London, for instance, teens join sports clubs or work at after-school jobs. Or maybe they will spend time with friends. Favorite pastimes in the afternoon and evening include attending concerts, going out for coffee, browsing through record stores or bookshops, and going to the movies.

Life is often quieter in the English countryside than it is in the cities. Rather than depending on public transportation, rural teens depend on their two feet. Teens often walk to school,

church, stores, and their friends' houses. After all, walking a couple of miles is nothing to most rural Britons.

Rural teens may have a number of daily chores to perform. For those who live on working farms, chores may include feeding and milking animals, cleaning barns and sheds, mowing lawns, clearing brush, mending fences, or helping to clean and fillet fish. The amount and types of chores that are done depend on a family's economic situation. However, nearly all teens are expected to keep their bedrooms clean

Most rural teens live in small towns rather than on working farms.

Going Places

In England, walking is the best way to go a couple of miles or less. To travel longer distances, or to travel short distances more quickly, public transportation is the way to go. In London, red double-decker buses run throughout the city. Travelers can catch a bus or the Tube every few minutes. In the suburbs, public transportation is a bit harder to find, though buses usually run every half or quarter hour in most towns.

English bus and train lines carry people across the country. Public transportation is fairly cheap, especially when compared with the price of petrol (gasoline) or the cost of a car. Many teens do not bother to learn how to drive until they need to get a car for work.

Cars are more common in families that live in the suburbs or in the country. Usually parents have at least one car that they let their teenagers occasionally borrow. People in England drive on the left side of the road, and cars are set up with the driver's seat on the right and the passenger on the left. Most cars in England are manual. The driver must use three pedals—accelerator, brake, and clutch—and shift gears.

Bicycles are also common in the countryside. Many teens, both city and country dwellers, save up to buy a motorized bike or a scooter. They find that it is much easier to park a scooter than a car. However, there is always a risk of scooters being stolen, especially in the cities.

Even though many teens do not drive, most eventually take their driving tests and get a license. The legal age for a driver's license is 17. The first step is taking a formal driving class. When they feel confident, teens take an exam that tests their understanding of traffic laws. A practical driving test follows. And if they do well enough, they earn a license.

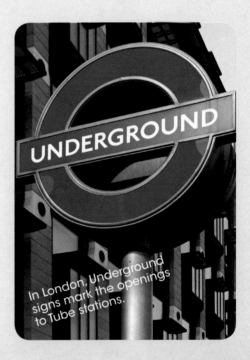

In London, Underground signs mark the openings to Tube stations.

and help out around the house. In families with toddlers, teens are often asked to help take care of the younger children, especially if one or both parents work long hours.

Rewards & Rules

Most English children—both urban and rural—receive an allowance, starting at about age 7. Depending on a family's financial situation, the allowance can range from less than 1 pound (about U.S.$2) to 10 pounds (about U.S.$20) a week. Allowances often go toward mobile-phone charges or are saved for purchases in a city center. Male teens often spend money on football gear and trainers (athletic shoes). Some hobbies, such as painting, require supplies, and kids save up for magazines and compact discs. Music, clothes, food, and movies are the most common expenses.

Younger teens often have curfews. The appointed time is usually earlier when school is in session. Most parents relax the rules a little in the summer and allow teens to stay out an hour or two later, as long as they still get all their chores done. Younger teens learn not to break curfew, since disobeying their parents may result in their allowances being cut or their being grounded. In many households, parents don't mind if their children stay out later, as long as they call home first.

Older teens are less dependent on their parents financially and therefore think that their parents shouldn't tell

In London, mobile phones have become more popular than the traditional red phone booths.

them when to come home at night. Once a teen gets a job or goes to a university, most parents feel that he or she has shown a sense of responsibility. They loosen curfews or even discard them completely. Teens over 17 usually can come and go as they please.

Homes & Houses

Home environments depend in large part on a family's financial situation. Wealthier families usually own country estates or houses, or city flats (apartments). Working-class families often have houses outside of a city, or they rent flats. Houses in cities are often made of brick and plaster and tend to be older, while most suburban houses were built in the last 50 years.

England is known for its gardens, a term that refers to grass yards, as well as flower and vegetable patches. Even city homes usually have small backyards, or gardens. High fences separate one garden from another. Many houses and apartments boast window boxes with flowers, herbs, and small vegetables. These are especially popular in apartments where a family does not have an individual garden.

In many families, teenagers have their own bedrooms. In others, they share a room with a sibling. Teens' bedrooms are often decorated with pictures of movie stars, musicians, sports figures, and other role models. Family pictures, snapshots of friends, and posters of vacation spots or movies

are also common. Some teens keep pets in their rooms.

Though teens are often nagged by their parents to keep their rooms clean, most ignore the message and leave their rooms a mess. For many teens, keeping a messy room is a way to rebel against their parents. Most become neater when they move out.

Pets in English Homes

Depending on where a family lives, pets can be very common. The English

English gardens combine formal, pruned bushes with natural-looking plots of flowers and grasses.

love their pets, especially dogs and cats. Terriers and spaniels are among the more common dog types, and there are always plenty of mutts. While children love strays, professional women and men usually prefer pure-bred animals.

In cities, people frequently walk their dogs along the streets or play fetch in the parks. Urban owners keep their cats indoors most of the time to minimize the risks of their becoming lost,

More than half of British families own a pet.

getting hit by cars, or fighting with stray cats. Fish (in both indoor tanks and outdoor ponds) are also common. Other easy-to-care-for animals include birds, small reptiles, and small mammals, such as rabbits and guinea pigs.

Families with dogs and cats sometimes have a separate room for the animals, but most owners allow them to roam through almost all the rooms of the house. During the day, dogs are usually kept outside. In the evening, dogs are brought inside, and cats are sent outside for a bit. Most families put food outside for their pets, and cats can jump into neighboring yards and help themselves to any leftovers. As a result, moggies, or alley cats, are usually well-fed. A stray moggy might even find a sympathetic family offering food on a regular basis.

Vet Turned Author

In 1966, an English country veterinarian began writing about his experiences with animals. James Alfred Wight was 50 years old when his writing career began. Using the pen name James Herriot, Wight wrote collections of stories. Eventually the tales formed books such as *All Creatures Great and Small* and *James Herriot's Dog Stories.* Two films and a long-running British television show, *All Creatures Great and Small,* brought the animal tales to the big and small screens.

In more rural areas, pets are usually expected to work. On farms, cats help their owners and satisfy their own predatory nature by keeping barns free of mice and other rodents. Collies and other herding dogs are used to drive sheep, and many dogs are used for hunting. Some rural pet owners discourage their children from playing too much with their hardworking animals. They fear that the pets will become spoiled.

More Than Just Fish & Chips

Most English teens love their native foods. Despite a common stereotype held outside of Britain, not everything the English eat is boiled. Some foods are steamed, stewed, or fried. Because no place in England is more than 75 miles (120 km) from the sea, many of the most popular dishes involve seafood.

In fact England's "national food" is fish and chips. Deep-fried fish, usually cod or haddock, is served with fried potato wedges (widely known as chips). Traditionally this dish was bought from a cart on a street or beach. It came in a newspaper cone and was eaten while walking around. Today restaurants usually serve it in waxed paper and provide forks. The proper, or at least most popular, seasoning for fish and chips is salt and malt vinegar. In pubs (restaurant-bars) in the north of England, fish and chips is usually eaten with mushy green peas.

Many people also enjoy a variety of shellfish. During the summer, steamed winkles (short for periwinkles, a type of snail), cockles and mussels (types of mollusks), and oysters are often sold from carts on streets and popular beaches. The steamed treats are wrapped in paper or served in small baskets. Many vendors give customers a pin to help pull the winkles from the shell.

Pubs and restaurants often promote their specialties on their outdoor signs.

Another favorite English food is the sandwich, also called a butty or sarnie. The sandwich was invented in England and later came to be eaten in countries around the world.

In England, puddings are not always for dessert. Some, such as Yorkshire pudding and black pudding, are part of the main meal. Yorkshire pudding is a baked egg, milk, and flour mixture, which is often served with a roast beef dinner. Black pudding is made of dried pig's blood and fat mixed with pork fat and stuffed into casings. It is often served at breakfast.

Pies are also served at all stages of the meal. Some, such as steak and kidney pie, have meat in them, while others are sweet and served for "afters," or dessert. The Cornish pasty contains a mix of meat, peas, potatoes or other tubers, and root vegetables, which are seasoned, wrapped in a pastry shell and baked. It ends up in a half-circle shape and makes a very filling meal. Another dish is star-gazy pie, a fish pie in which several whole herring are fanned out, with their heads facing outward. The pastry shell is laid on top, and the edge is peeled back in spots to show the fish gazing upward.

Interestingly, none of these dishes is as popular as curry. This dish was imported from India. It first became popular among the English in the 1800s, when England ruled India. Hundreds of types of curry are served in England. Some are meat-based, some vegetarian, and some are very hot, while others are less spicy or almost sweet. Many teens go out for curry at their favorite local eating spot

Roast beef dinner, complete with Yorkshire pudding (top left), is often served on Sundays.

Curry can be eaten in restaurants, ordered for delivery, or purchased from an outdoor vendor. Many English also make their own version at home.

before heading to the pub or to a show.

The English often drink black tea or alcohol at dinner. Although most English drink sweet, milky tea as young people, many adults prefer their tea with less milk and sometimes without sugar. However it is fixed, tea is drunk at every meal, and many people take an

A Diverse Nation

England is a multicultural society, which helps explain the diverse menus. Its people come from a range of cultural, national, racial, and religious backgrounds. This diversity reaches back into England's early history. When Romans conquered Britain in 43 A.D., a new culture was introduced. This was followed by invaders from Northern Europe.

Later England was viewed as a welcoming place for those trying to escape poor conditions in their own countries. In 1789, for example, a group of refugees from the French Revolution arrived. In the 1800s, Jewish settlers immigrated to get away from persecution in Poland and Russia. Irish settlers arrived after a famine in Ireland in the 1840s led to major poverty. Then in the 1960s, immigrants from Bangladesh, India, and Pakistan began coming to England. They pursued work in textiles and other industries.

Other minority groups include people from the Caribbean Islands, South Africa, and the Middle East. All of these ethnicities combine to form a very complex national identity. Minorities make up an estimated 7 percent of the population. That number is expected to double by 2020. In major cities, the diversity is, of course, even greater. One-third of Londoners, for example, were born outside of the country.

Many English people are proud of this diverse background. In a 2001 speech, Prime Minister Tony Blair spoke about it: "We celebrate the diversity in our country, get strength from the cultures and the races that go to make up Britain today."

afternoon or evening tea, as well.

Afternoon tea is a tradition that was started in 1840 by a duchess in Bedford. She regularly became hungry at 4 P.M., but her dinner was not served until 8. Tea with cakes and sandwiches provided a snack. Soon she began inviting her friends to join her, and the custom spread.

Today most families do not have time for a formal tea with all the trimmings. However, many people keep the tradition of having a cup of tea and a snack. Crumpets, flat, pancakelike muffins with lots of holes, are eaten hot with plenty of butter.

Traditionally, coffee was not widely consumed in England. However, with the rise of coffee shops such as Starbucks, it is growing in popularity. Students especially depend on the caffeinated beverage to get them through hours of studying.

Children and teenagers do not usually drink milk with meals, though it is common to use milk on breakfast cereals, including Weetabix (a brand

Cups and saucers and matching tea pots make for a proper tea setting.

Teens & Alcohol

Partly because their parents allow them to drink beer and wine at home, many English teens become fond of alcoholic beverages. Alcohol Concern is an English agency that addresses the problems of alcohol abuse. According to the agency, 90 percent of youths ages 15 and 16 have had alcohol at least once. Forty-three percent have consumed alcohol at least 40 times. For some teens, drinking alcohol can become a serious problem. An Alcohol Concern 2004 study showed that 54 percent of 15- and 16-year-olds have engaged in binge drinking, consuming more than five drinks in a single occasion. Some teens see drinking as a way to rebel. But many simply see it as something they want to do.

How Often Do Teens Drink?
Frequency of Drinking Among 11- to 15-Year-Olds

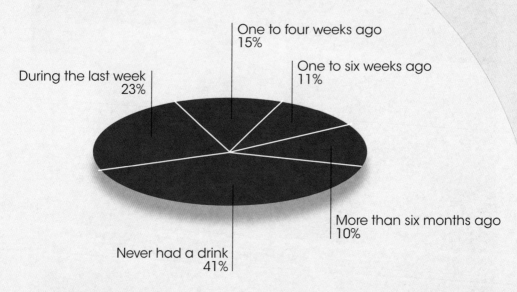

One to four weeks ago
15%

One to six weeks ago
11%

During the last week
23%

More than six months ago
10%

Never had a drink
41%

Source: Alcohol Concern. *Young People's Drinking Fact Sheet: Summary.* November 2005.

What's for Dinner?

English menus feature unique names for dishes. Here are a few:

bangers and mash—sausage and mashed potato

bubble and squeak—potatoes and cabbage

Marmite—a spread for toast made from brewer's yeast extract

neeps and tatties—potatoes and turnips

spotted dick—steamed dough with raisins in it

toad in the hole—meat (usually sausage) wrapped in batter and cooked

tripe—a cow's stomach lining, boiled with onions

of cereal) and porridge (oatmeal).

As for alcohol, the legal drinking age in England is 18. However, parents are allowed to serve their children alcohol in the privacy of their homes. Most parents won't give their children cocktails and other hard liquor until they are at least 18. But teens sometimes drink beer or wine with their meals.

Many English desserts are made fresh in the family kitchen. Most bread in England has no preservatives and spoils quickly. Bread pudding is a way of using up old bread before it goes bad. This mixture of bread, eggs, and milk is usually flavored with cinnamon and raisins or currants. Other favorite desserts include milk and egg custards, fresh fruit, and frozen yogurt. Teens also buy sweets and candies for snacks during the day. Some teens stop by small bakeries to pick up biscuits (cookies) or an almond or chocolate croissant.

Grocery stores carry a variety of chocolate bars, another teen favorite. Cadbury is a popular brand of chocolates. The brand offers candies such as Dairy Milk, Aero, Flake, Hero, and Turkish Delight. Other sweets include an Australian import called Violet Crumble. This spongelike candy is covered in chocolate, which is supposed to be shattered before it is eaten. Toffees, such as Mackintosh, must be snapped before being chewed.

English teens can depend on their friends for support and fun.

3

Changes in Family Life

THE MAKEUP OF FAMI- LIES IN ENGLAND HAS CHANGED SIGNIFICANTLY IN RECENT DECADES. About 70 percent of UK families are considered traditional. These families are headed by a married couple. Families headed by just one parent or by an unmarried couple living together have become increasingly common.

Statistics show that British views on marriage and family have changed. Both divorce and cohabitation are widely accepted. Living together is an option for some young adults who choose not to make their union legal. Today about 11 percent of dependent children in the United Kingdom live with parents who are not married. In addition, single parenthood was once frowned upon by most people. Today it is becoming more socially acceptable. About 24 percent of children are growing up in single-parent households.

Small families are the norm in England. The average UK family size is estimated at 1.6 children. A family's social background, religion, and financial situation play important roles in determining

Where Children Live

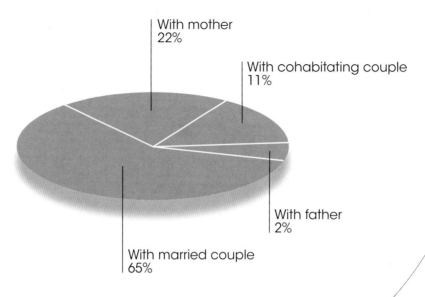

With mother
22%

With cohabitating couple
11%

With father
2%

With married couple
65%

Source: National Statistics.

its size. In general, the lower a family's economic status, the more children are born. Most English families have between one and five children.

On Their Own

Because the traditional nuclear family is not as common as in the past, the traditional extended family has become less important in England. Teens are still likely to spend holidays with their aunts, uncles, cousins, and grandparents.

However, this sort of family time is generally not a high priority within the culture.

Following suit, teens do not depend on their parents as much as young people in other European countries do. A 2006 study by the Institute for Public Policy Research in England found that only 64 percent of British 15-year-olds eat regularly with their families. In comparison, 93 percent of Italian teenagers eat with their families on a regular basis. The same study also found that 45 percent of 15-year-old British boys spent most evenings away from home, hanging out with friends.

In France, by comparison, the number is 17 percent.

Though England's teens often feel comfortable talking with their parents, the culture encourages young people to become independent in many ways. Teens do not have to depend on their parents to teach them life's lessons. Schools cover topics such as sex education, and the government provides a number of services to address other topics, ranging from career advice to travel guides.

Perhaps because this independence is fostered at a young age, it is not uncommon for teens to move out of their parents' houses by the age of 16 or 17. Sometimes they feel they are grown up enough to strike out on their own. In other cases, they are attending a university in a distant town or another country. Or perhaps they have found a good job in another town. In any case, young people who have found a well-paying job or are married

Teens often prepare their own meals and eat separately from their parents and siblings.

are expected to find their own houses or apartments. For these reasons, most young people leave their parents' homes for good by age 20.

When teens decide to leave home, they are likely to live near family, as long as they remain in England. England is a small country, especially when compared with huge nations like Russia, Canada, and the United States. It rarely takes longer than five hours to get from one point in England to another. As a result, English teens and young adults who live on their own are able to visit their parents and siblings fairly frequently. They are further aided by England's reliable railroad system, which serves all parts of the country.

Expense Report

Roughly 10 percent of English families have a child over age 20 still living at home. This is due in part to the high cost of living in England, especially in the cities. For instance, the cost of renting a one-room flat in London, is between 110 pounds (U.S.$217) and 160 pounds (U.S.$315) per week. By living with their parents a bit longer than they'd like, young people can save up their money. This is especially helpful when they are just starting out in the working world. They still have plenty of expenses. Here's a look at what the British pay for a few items:

Kit Kat candy bar	0.48 pounds (U.S.95 cents)
Can of Pepsi	0.60 pounds (U.S.$1.18)
McDonald's meal	4.50 pounds (U.S.$8.86)
Cinema (movie) ticket	7.50 pounds (U.S.$14.78)
Ride on the London Tube	1.30 pounds (U.S.$2.56)

What's in a Name?

In England, parents' family backgrounds play a large part in naming children. As in other English-speaking countries, a person's name consists of the given name (first name), one or more middle names, and the family surname (last name).

Given names in England come from many sources. Children may be named after an ancestor or a favorite relative as an honor to a family member. Or a mother's maiden name may become a child's middle name, so that family heritage is not lost. Other parents choose names based on how they sound or how well they fit with a last name. Some parents name children after a personal hero, a celebrity, or an important place or event.

Though names such as Faith or Constance are occasionally seen, most English names do not hold any special meaning. The roots of the words have

Name That Baby

In 2006, the most popular baby names in England for boys and girls were:

	Boys	Girls
1.	Jack	Olivia
2.	Thomas	Grace
3.	Joshua	Jessica
4.	Oliver	Ruby
5.	Harry	Emily
6.	James	Sophie
7.	William	Chloe
8.	Samuel	Lucy
9.	Daniel	Lily
10.	Charlie	Ellie

In 1998, they were:

	Boys	Girls
1.	Jack	Olivia
2.	Thomas	Emily
3.	James	Megan
4.	Daniel	Jessica
5.	Joshua	Sophie
6.	Matthew	Charlotte
7.	Samuel	Hannah
8.	Callum	Lauren
9.	Joseph	Rebecca
10.	Jordan	Lucy

Jack was the most popular boy's name in England for 12 years in a row!

been lost in history. So while most names do have meanings (for instance, Sophie means "wisdom"), most people are unaware of those meanings.

A Second Family

Because teens tend to be independent from their families at a young age, friendships become very important in England. Teens usually have at least a

Friends at boarding schools can hang out in each other's rooms during free time.

Teen Slang

Teens have their own set of words that may confuse the adults in their lives. Slang is always changing, so it can be hard to keep up with the words and their meanings.

buff — attractive, fit
hangin — ugly and badly dressed
howling — ugly
kotch — chill out
lush — good-looking
rents — parents
snog — kiss

few friends from school, from the neighborhood, or from involvement in various academic or athletic clubs. In boarding schools, students often find friends within their dormitories. Some teens only see their friends at school. Others get together with schoolmates on Saturdays to hang out or go to parties.

Emma, who lived in Kent (a county southeast of London), went to an all-girls school. She explained:

"I had a few friends in the neighbor-hood, but I wouldn't usually see school friends until the next day. Maybe we would meet up on a Saturday to stroll the town and shopping centers, but that was about it. There weren't any after-school activities at my senior school either. The doors shut at 3:30 every day! You would get in trouble for loitering after that."

Another way English teens hang out is to have sleepovers. These parties are especially popular on weekends. Participants can stay up most of the night without having to worry about school in the morning. The sleepovers involve teens of the same gender and are usually small, with five or six teens at most.

House parties are another big part of teenage life. The get-togethers are especially popular after teens turn 16. At this age, many teens are finished with school and have paying jobs. Rob, a teenager from Exeter, a city in the south-western county of Devon, says:

"Most younger teenagers don't really

have house parties other than maybe for a birthday. Older teenagers have house parties more often."

In cities, teenagers also go clubbing. Dancing and live music are very popular, and a nightclub is a common place to meet new friends. In addition, teenagers can meet potential boyfriends and girlfriends almost anywhere—in stores or cafes, at work or during classes, even at the grocery store. The dates themselves often take place at clubs, cafes, restaurants, parks, sporting arenas, or the movies.

As with young people in other countries, dating is a complex issue for English teens. Some take dating more seriously and will only go out with

Fitting In

Commonly, teens feel intense pressure to have an attractive body or the right attitude. They read magazines and see movies filled with so-called ideal images. Younger teens, says Rob, the teen from Exeter, don't worry too much about following fashions, but older teens are much more self-conscious. Many teens are teased mercilessly in school. Some teens find themselves fitting in by drinking or smoking with their friends.

Twenty percent of teens in the United Kingdom are regular smokers. Since smoking can lead to illnesses such as cancer, heart disease, and respiratory problems, the British Medical Association is greatly concerned about the historically high tobacco use among teens. The association has made recommendations to the government on how to make cigarettes harder for teens to buy. Dr. Vivienne Nathanson, BMA head of science and ethics, said:

"Forcing shops selling cigarettes to have a license ... would be a public recognition of the dangers of tobacco. Cigarettes aren't like milk or bread, where anyone can and should be able to sell them. Cigarettes aren't as dangerous as guns, but they kill more people than alcohol or guns in the UK. ... We need to change the culture of cigarette-buying by recognizing that."

In London, young friends may take part in a new fad called mobile clubbing. Participants are told where and when to meet via their mobile phones. When the destination is reached, they dance to music of their own choice on MP3 players.

people they could imagine marrying. Others prefer a more casual approach and hang out with a variety of people. And as with all teenagers, those who are going steady worry about how their friends will get along with their boyfriends and girlfriends.

Festivals and other celebrations bring out English people of all ages and backgrounds.

4

A Festive Country

THE ENGLISH LOVE ANY EXCUSE TO HAVE A GOOD TIME. There are more than 70 national celebrations and holidays each year. In addition, individual towns and cities hold their own festivals. There are celebrations of regional heroes, historic events, community togetherness, and local characters.

In Stratford on Avon, for instance, each April brings a weekend of festivities in honor of playwright William Shakespeare's birthday. Shakespeare was born in the historic town in 1564. Celebrations include a birthday luncheon with toasts to the author and a performance of one of his plays.

Another popular local celebration is the Gloucestershire tradition called cheese rolling. The event is believed to be a pre-Roman tradition. A 7-pound (3.15-kilogram) wheel of double Gloucester cheese is rolled down an extremely steep hill, with many competitors chasing after it. There are almost always injuries, such as sprained ankles, cut heads, and scraped knees, when people lose their balance and tumble down the hill. What does the winner get? The winner gets to keep the cheese!

Bank Holidays

National holidays in England are referred to as bank holidays. Banks are not allowed to operate on these days, and most of England enjoys a day off. England's bank holidays include:

New Year's Day—January 1

Good Friday—March or April

Easter Monday—March or April

May Day—First Monday in May

Spring Bank Holiday—Last Monday in May

Summer Bank Holiday—Last Monday in August

Christmas Day—December 25

Boxing Day—December 26

Happy Holidays

While many English families don't practice a religion, one of England's most popular holidays is religious in

nature. Christmas, the celebration of Jesus Christ's birth, is December 25. The English begin preparing for the big day a few weeks ahead of time. They decorate, send cards to friends, and buy and wrap gifts. In some places, teens go caroling with their families. Most English cities have Christmas parades and festivals,

Harrods department store in London is a favorite spot for Christmas shopping.

57

Faith & Religion

England is officially a Christian country, and the British monarch serves as the head of the Church of England. However, citizens have religious freedoms. A number of other faiths, including Islam, Hinduism, Sikhism, and Judaism, are practiced throughout the country.

Nearly 72 percent of the population identify themselves as Christian. But religion plays a small part in the lives of most English teenagers. Most Protestant teens find themselves in church for weddings, funerals, and some holidays only. Many young people and their parents do not attend religious services regularly.

Others find religion to be a large part of their lives. Second to Protestants, Roman Catholics make up the next largest religious group in England. Many Catholic teens go to Mass with their families. Followers of other minority religions, such as Islam, also tend to be more devout.

"For some," says an English woman named Jay, "religion is important all of their lives, but for many, it [the teenage years] is a time at which the questions started to get asked." Teens often find themselves looking outside of religion for answers about life. Many are spiritual, but they prefer a less formal approach to religious devotion. These teens sometimes experiment with more than one religion before finding a road to spirituality that works for them.

Some teens become very devout, but many people don't know what their friends' religions are. Emma, who grew up in Kent, says that it's "not to say folks aren't religious or spiritual. It's just not discussed too much generally."

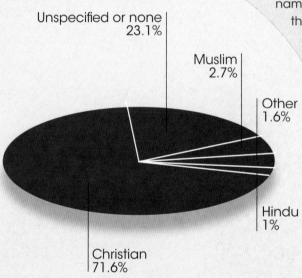

Unspecified or none
23.1%

Muslim
2.7%

Other
1.6%

Hindu
1%

Christian
71.6%

Source: United States Central Intelligence Agency. *The World Factbook—United Kingdom.*

and many shops keep extended hours for last-minute shopping.

More English people attend church services on Christmas Day than on any other day of the year. Extended-family members often gather to eat a traditional Christmas dinner. Roast turkey and potatoes, Brussels sprouts, cranberry sauce, bread stuffing, small sausages wrapped in bacon, and gravy make up the menu. The meal is followed by Christmas pudding—a bread pudding with dried fruit and nuts served with custard or a sauce made with brandy, a type of alcohol. Guests enjoy opening Christmas crackers. These tubes of paper hold a paper crown and a small token inside. Partners each pull at one of the twisted ends to make the tube "crack" and spill its surprises.

The day after Christmas is Boxing Day. This traditional holiday dates to the 1200s. No one is sure about the origins of the day. One explanation is that it marked the day when the church alms boxes were opened. The money inside was given to the poor. Another story says that because servants were often required to work on Christmas Day, they would get the following day off to visit their families. The employers would present the servants with Christmas "boxes" filled with food and other gifts. Today Boxing Day is spent playing games and watching sports as a family.

Other favorite holidays for teens include Halloween and Guy Fawkes Night. Halloween festivities for older teens include dressing up in costumes,

Extended families gather for Christmas dinner. The Christmas crackers are placed in the middle of the table.

Teens like to choose scary or flirty costumes for Halloween.

going to big parties, and staying out late. Younger teens and children enjoy carving jack-o'-lanterns, going trick-or-treating, and eating too much candy.

Guy Fawkes Night, or Bonfire Night, is one of the most popular of all English holidays. The holiday remembers Guy Fawkes, the famous traitor who planned to blow up the houses of Parliament in 1605 with a raft loaded

with barrels of gunpowder. Though his plan failed, it is remembered in rhyme: *Remember, remember, the fifth of November, Gunpowder treason and plot, I see no reason why gunpowder treason Should ever be forgot!*

The holiday falls on November 5 and is celebrated with huge bonfires all over the country. One woman says, "Giant, dangerous bonfires are especially fun as a teen—the bigger the better!" Teens also delight in burning "Guy" in effigy. Groups gather at the bonfires, where potatoes, soup, and sausages can be cooked at the edge of the flames. Fireworks are set off once it gets dark.

Some communities celebrate Guy Fawkes Night with parades through town.

Celebrations in All Seasons

There are major festivals throughout the year. New Year's Day, the first of January, is celebrated by making resolutions for the year to come. Teens stay up late the night before to welcome the new year at midnight.

February 14 is St. Valentine's Day. This is traditionally seen as the first day of spring. In Sussex (a county in southeast England), Valentine's Day is called the Birds' Wedding Day. According to tradition, the identity of a girl's future husband can be foretold by what bird she sees first on Valentine's Day. A robin means that she will marry a sailor, a goldfinch that she will find a rich man, and a sparrow that she will be happy with a poor man.

In the spring, newborn lambs and daffodils are seen in the fields. The weather is pleasant, usually between 55 and 68 degrees Fahrenheit (13 and 20 degrees Celsius). In March, St. Piran's Day honors the patron saint of Cornwall, who is credited with discovering tin. (In ancient times, tin mined in England was exported throughout Europe and combined with copper to produce bronze. This was perhaps the most widely used metal then.)

April 1 is April Fool's Day. This is a day when teens play practical jokes on each other. Such jokes must be played before noon, otherwise the joke is on the trickster! In May, the blossoms come out and the temperature rises to 70 F (21 C). In a number of towns in the countryside, performances of Morris dancing—a colorful English folk dance dating from medieval times—are presented on May Day, the first of May. It is a celebration of winter's end.

In June, roses are blooming in most parts of England. The temperature is a lovely 75 or 80 F (24 or 27 C), and it is rarely humid. Many families take part in outdoor activities and theater and musical performances.

June is also the month for the Ascot horse races. On opening day, men arrive in tuxedos and women are dressed up in gowns with long gloves and beautiful hats. Many celebrities attend the Royal Ascot, the set of races frequently attended by members of the nobility. Tabloids and magazines are full of pictures of their outfits, especially their hats.

July and August are hotter months than June and have fewer holidays. Many towns have their own carnivals at this time. The Notting Hill Carnival in London is held in late August. Parades, street festivals, and traveling musicians and dancers entertain crowds of people.

Fall has its share of holidays, too. September brings blustery winds and beautiful autumn leaves, as well as a number of colorful harvest festivals, to many parts of England. The teen favorites Halloween and Guy Fawkes Night follow.

Morris dancers wave handkerchiefs or sticks as part of the dance on May Day.

Personal Holidays

Personal events such as births, birthdays, weddings, and deaths are also honored in England. Births, for example, are announced in local newspapers. Some families hold small gatherings when the baby arrives home. Baby showers before the birth are becoming more popular. They are a good way for women to socialize and get advice about pregnancy and child rearing.

The English honor birthdays with gifts. The birthday boy or girl opens them as soon as he or she pops out of bed. When children are young, they often invite friends from school to their house for parties, with cake and games. More often than not, English teens celebrate their birthdays by going out with a few friends. The most important birthday to celebrate is the 18th, when teens are legally allowed to vote and drink alcohol. Sometimes the party is a huge event, complete with a sound system and party lights.

Love & Marriage

Weddings provide another reason to

As is common in Western cultures, candles—one for each year of life—cover the birthday cake.

Though church weddings are still the most common, more couples are choosing to wed in nonreligious ceremonies.

celebrate. Many Western wedding traditions got their start in England. The custom of brides wearing white, for instance, began when Queen Victoria (who reigned from 1837 to 1901) chose to be wed in white as a symbol of purity.

An English wedding celebration begins on the way to the ceremony location. The bride and her wedding party are led by a young girl who scatters flower petals along the way. The petals are symbolic of creating a happy path in life.

Most weddings in England are held in a church. After the ceremony, guests toss colorful confetti or rice at the new couple. This tradition hails from the 17th century, when wheat was thrown at brides as they left the church. A reception starts with a meal called the wedding breakfast, though most weddings take place at noon. Dancing often follows.

Bookstore employees prepared Harry Potter books for sale. The service industry, which includes retail, employs 80 percent of UK work...

5

Finding a Place in the Adult World

IN ENGLAND, WORK BECOMES A PART OF LIFE AT A YOUNG AGE. Many teens start working at part-time jobs when they are 13 years old, the legal age of employment. Typical work includes delivering newspapers, baby-sitting, and doing farmwork. Because the national minimum wage doesn't apply to workers under 16, most of these jobs do not pay very well. Nonetheless, most offer good experience, especially if a teen makes a good impression. Knowing the right people and having a good working reputation are helpful when a teen looks for a full-time job.

Many English people become full-time workers by the age of 16 or 17. When teens enter the job world, they often want to be considered adults. Adult co-workers' views of teenage workers depend on the job. A teenager who gets a job at a fast-food restaurant is less likely to be treated as an adult. Most inexpensive restaurants have short labor turnover times—that is, employees don't often stay at the job for more than a few months or a year. Short jobs like these are usually not thought of as serious jobs.

In contrast, serious jobs include positions as bank clerks, insurance salespeople, engineers, or computer specialists. These positions often provide better pay and opportunities for advancement. In these jobs, teens tend to be treated with more respect. They may even have as many opportunities as adults.

Choosing a Path

For young people in England, the process of finding a promising first serious

What's Minimum Wage?

England's minimum hourly wage—the least employers can pay by law—varies according to the age of the employee.

Age	Wage
16-18	3.30 pounds (U.S.$6.50)
18-21	4.45 pounds (U.S.$8.77)
22 and older	5.35 pounds (U.S.$10.55)

Source: United Kingdom Department of Trade and Industry, 2007.

Many young people hope to enter the often high-paying world of banking and finance.

job often begins in school. Career specialists visit schools to give aptitude tests and provide career advice. Of course, the decision to follow that advice is entirely up to the individual.

When young people enter the working world, they will likely work in England's service industry. About 80 percent of UK workers have positions in fields such as medicine, hotel and restaurant management, or retail. Also included in the service industries are banking and insurance, which are of major importance to the English economy. London is home to the Bank of England (the national bank), the London Stock Exchange, and Lloyd's (an international insurance organization). The city

Division of Labor

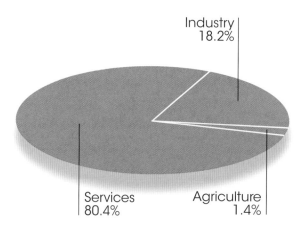

Industry
18.2%

Services
80.4%

Agriculture
1.4%

Source: United States Central Intelligence Agency.
The World Factbook—United Kingdom.

is an international financial center.

Even teens fresh out of school can get a job in this business world. At age 16, Kent native Emma Ulrich got a job with an insurance company in a very busy financial district. She worked as a receptionist and completed data entry. After four months, she considered the work atmosphere horrible. Then she was thrilled to receive a first-year Christmas bonus of about 2,500 pounds (U.S.$5,000).

Another 18 percent of the work-force is employed in heavy industry and manufacturing. In the late 1800s, England became one of the first industrialized nations. Many factories developed and expanded. Cities such as Manchester and Birmingham saw major growth. As investing and bank-ing have grown in importance, manu-facturing has declined. However, heavy industry still accounts for more than 25 percent of the United Kingdom's gross domestic product.

Few English teens enter work in agriculture, which employs just over 1 percent of the workforce. As farm machinery and techniques have advanced, the number of people employed in farming has declined. Despite the small employment numbers, the agriculture industry provides 60 percent of England's food needs. Major products include the grains

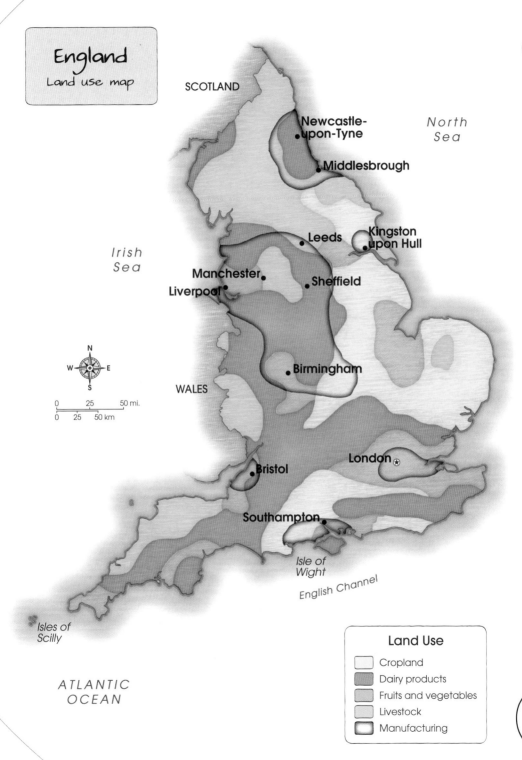

England
Land use map

SCOTLAND

North
Sea

Newcastle-
upon-Tyne
Middlesbrough

Irish
Sea

Leeds
Kingston
upon Hull

Manchester
Liverpool
Sheffield

Birmingham

WALES

N
W   E
S

0   25   50 mi.
0   25   50 km

London

Bristol

Southampton

Isle of
Wight

English Channel

Isles of
Scilly

ATLANTIC
OCEAN

Land Use

Cropland
Dairy products
Fruits and vegetables
Livestock
Manufacturing

71

wheat, barley, and oats; vegetables such as potatoes and sugar beets; and livestock such as cattle, chicken, and sheep. Cod, haddock, and mackerel are among the important fishing products.

Military Service & Civic Duty

When neither the job world nor a university degree seems right, a teen may decide to enter the military. Teens also join the military because they have a sense of duty or national pride. Military service is voluntary. There is no draft in England, and teens do not have to register for selective service. They can join the British Army at age 16 with their parents' consent. After they reach 18, they no longer need permission.

One military path is the Royal Military Police. This armed force helps

All army soldiers receive basic training in field operations, weapon handling, and physical fitness.

Prince William (rear) and Prince Harry often attend military ceremonies with their father, Prince Charles, and his wife, Camilla.

A Royal Affair

Traditionally, members of England's royal family have served in the military. Prince Charles, heir to the throne, is a trained pilot with the Royal Air Force and enlisted in the Royal Navy. In 2005 his sons, William and Harry, also joined the military. Both enlisted in the British Army.

In 2006, William was made a second lieutenant in the Household Cavalry. Harry holds the same position, in addition to being an officer in the British Army.

with security patrols, crime prevention and investigation, traffic and riot control, and assisting the civil police in other duties in London and other cities.

Teens and young adults can also sign up for combat roles in the infantry, the Royal Air Force (RAF), the Household Cavalry, and the Royal Armored Corps. Teens who opt for military careers also obtain job skills. They can learn about engineering, information technology, electronics, supply management, dog training, and even music. In addition, those with an interest in health care can work in a number of military-related fields. The military needs combat medics, veterinarians, dentists, and pharmacists, to name a few.

For most English teens, free time is likely spent with friends.

6

Free Time on the Island

LIKE MANY EUROPEANS, THE ENGLISH ENJOY THEIR BREAKS FROM THE DAILY GRIND. They are sure to vacation or simply relax close to home on a regular basis. The majority of a teen's free time is spent with friends. If teens can get transportation, they go to theme parks with groups of friends. Going to a pub for dinner and playing pool or darts are common both in cities and in the countryside. Another favorite hangout for kids as young as 14 is a club. Different clubs feature different kinds of music, and many teens go out to hear favorite local bands.

Shopping provides a quieter public pastime. On Sundays, shops are not open as late as on other days, but shopping then is still an enjoyable leisure activity. Many teens don't buy anything. Instead they just like to look at the new fashions and hang out with their friends. A trip to the movies is another favorite activity. Many American actors and actresses—as well as Hollywood itself—are popular in England.

To relax, teens often gather at a friend's house or flat. They might play cards or

A Sporting Good Time

In both cities and the country, English teens are often involved in sports, mostly through school, but sometimes in informal clubs. Among the most popular sports for teens are football (soccer), rugby, and tennis.

Cricket, the precursor of baseball, is also an extremely popular sport in England. It is played on grass fields with two 11-person teams competing. The sport comes with its own set of slang. Here are a few examples:

all rounder
good at both batting and bowling (throwing); good at all positions

baggy green
the large green cap that Australian cricketers wear

beamer
a ball bowled (thrown) at the batsman's head

cherry
a new ball (which is bright red)

duck
a score of zero

flannels
the white or cream-colored outfit worn by cricketers

gardening
when a batsman pats down loose dirt with his bat

jaffa
a perfect pitch or an unhittable ball

notch
a run (games were first scored by cutting notches into wood)

pie thrower
a poor-quality bowler

sledge
to taunt an opponent

board games, or just talk and listen to music.

Pack Your Bags

Teens from all parts of England frequently take long day trips with their friends. The country's extensive train and bus systems make it easy to get almost anywhere in England in only a few hours. Some teens take the train into a big city on free days. Others take trips out of the cities to the beach, including Brighton. This southern seaside city has long been a popular getaway spot. It is often a stop on hit concert tours. Hordes of teens descend

Brighton is home to popular beaches and tourist attractions, such as amusement park rides.

BRIGHTON PIER

England
Topographical
map

River Tweed

SCOTLAND

North Sea

Cheviot Hills

Pennine Chain

Cumbrian Mountains

Scafell Pike ▲
Lake District

River Ouse

North Yorkshire Dales

Windermere

Irish Sea

Manchester •

Peak District

River Trent

The Fens

WALES

River Severn

Birmingham •

Great Ouse

River

River Wye

Salisbury Plain

River Thames

Bristol •

London ✪

White Cliffs of Dover

FRANCE

Brighton •

Isle of Wight

Seven Sisters

Cornish Riviera

English Channel

Isles of Scilly

ATLANTIC OCEAN

0   25   50 mi.
0   25   50 km

N W E S

━━ Major railroad

Lake Windermere is a favorite spot for water sports, such as kayaking.

on the city for weekend getaways.

Other teens travel north to the Lake District, in the northwestern section of England. Set in the Cumbrian Mountains, the area's rugged green valleys were made famous by English poets of the 19th century. Today teens enjoy hiking and fishing in the area.

Scotland and Wales are also easily accessible. There are no customs to go through at the borders of these regions because they are part of the United Kingdom. A visit to another portion of the United Kingdom, Northern Ireland, takes more planning. The popular destination lies across the Irish Sea from England's western coast. Getting to Northern Ireland requires boarding an airplane or ferry.

In addition to traveling with friends, teens often vacation with their families on mini-breaks of two or three days. On these holidays (vacations), families might go to another part of the country, visit relatives, or enjoy the seaside. The far western coast of England in Cornwall is so pleasant that it is known as the Cornish Riviera. This is a reference to the pleasant French Riviera, on France's Mediterranean coast. Along the southwest coast of Devon and Cornwall, it seems like springtime all year long. The weather never gets too hot, and the sun shines warmly on the beaches and the chalk cliffs.

Many natives of England also try to travel out of the country as often as they can. France and Spain are among the more popular foreign destinations. Teens who travel to these lands invariably encounter other cultures, languages, and customs. Frequent travelers tend to gain a broad understanding of the rest of the world.

England's Animal Kingdom

While traveling in England, teens become very familiar with a number of animals. Some of the more common are songbirds and small mammals. The English robin, a sparrow-sized bird, is seen year-round. Magpies are also common in England, especially in parks and fields. They are large birds, related to crows and jays, and display striking contrasts in their coloring and very long, dark tails.

In the English countryside, horses are a common sight, both in fields and on the road. Deer appear frequently as well. Smaller animals are often seen, such as badgers waddling across fields. Similar to a raccoon in size, a badger has black and white stripes down its muzzle and lives mainly underground. In years past, farmers killed badgers because it was commonly believed that they spread disease to cattle. However, the UK government has protected badgers by making it illegal to kill or injure the animals.

Another common small animal inhabiting the English countryside is the hedgehog. The shy mammals

Badgers come from the same mammal family as ferrets, weasels, and otters.

live mainly in hedges, or large thorn bushes. They have long noses and spikelike hairs across their backs. When in danger, the animal curls up into a little ball, spikes pointed outward, for protection. Unlike porcupine quills, hedgehogs' spikes will not puncture flesh.

On the Home Front

When they are not traveling, English teens spend their free time doing all sorts of activities. Many play video-games or watch the telly (television) after school. But not all teens have televisions, since each household has to pay a fee to have TV service. The current yearly cost is about 116 pounds (U.S. $232). The two British Broadcasting Corporation (BBC) channels do not run commercials, though the other three main television channels do. More channels are added by satellite. The English enjoy watching reality television, do-it-yourself shows, soap operas, and prime-time dramas and sitcoms.

Many teens are avid readers. And as Internet speeds get faster, more and more teens are spending time online. They blog, chat on the Net, keep up with friends on MySpace, and play interactive computer games.

Beloved Books

When the BBC polled English young people to find out what their favorite novels were in 2003, the results were a mix of classic and contemporary books. Here are some of the most popular:

Alice's Adventures in Wonderland, by Lewis Carroll

Anne of Green Gables, by Lucy Maud Montgomery

The BFG, by Roald Dahl

Black Beauty, by Anna Sewell

Charlie and the Chocolate Factory, by Roald Dahl

Double Act, by Jacqueline Wilson

Goodnight Mister Tom, by Michelle Magorian

The Harry Potter series, by J.K. Rowling

The Hobbit, by J.R.R. Tolkien

Holes, by Louis Sachar

The Lion, the Witch and the Wardrobe, by C. S. Lewis

Little Women, by Louisa May Alcott

Lord of the Flies, by William Golding

The Princess Diaries, by Meg Cabot

The Secret Garden, by Frances Hodgson Burnett

Treasure Island, by Robert Louis Stevenson

The entertainment magazine Hello! is a favorite among all ages.

Looking Ahead

ENGLAND'S TEENS ARE MORE INDEPENDENT THAN MANY EUROPEAN TEENS. Often young people are earning their own livings and supporting themselves. Concern about teen alcohol and drug abuse is growing. Meanwhile, family life in England is becoming less important in day-to-day life. However, young people form tight bonds with their friends, who provide them with support.

Though many teens enjoy relaxing at a house party or down at the local pub, they are hard workers. Students are dedicated to selecting and excelling in classes that will serve them in the future. Full-time workers are often supporting themselves and climbing career ladders. No matter what they do, England's youth is preparing to lead the country further into the 21st century. Living in one of Europe's wealthiest nations, they have a bright future.

At a Glance

Official name: England

Capital: London

People

Population: 50,100,000

Population by age group:
0–15 years: 19.7%
16–64 years: 64.4%
65 years and up: 15.9%

Life expectancy at birth: 79.05 years

Official language: English

Religions:
Note: The following data applies to the United Kingdom in its entirety.
Christian: 71.6%
Muslim: 2.7%
Hindu: 1%
Other: 1.6%
Unspecified or none: 23.1%

Legal ages
Alcohol consumption: 18
Driver's license: 17
Employment: 13
Marriage: 16 (with parental consent)
Military service: 16
Voting: 18

Government

Type of government in the UK:
Constitutional monarchy

Chief of state: Monarch

Head of government: Prime minister

Lawmaking body: Parliament consisting of the House of Lords and the elected House of Commons

Administrative divisions: 36 English counties

Independence: Unified in the 10th century

National symbols:
National flower: Rose
Patron saint: St. George
National animal: Lion

Geography

Total Area: 52,366 square miles (130,915 sq km)

Climate: Temperate; more than half of days are overcast

Highest point: Scafell Pike, 3,210 feet (979 meters)

Lowest point: The Fens, 13 feet (4 meters) below sea level

Major rivers: Ouse, Severn, Thames, Trent, Tweed, Wye

Major lake: Lake Windermere

Major landforms: Cheviot Hills, Cumbrian Mountains, North Yorkshire Dales, the Pennines, Salsbury Plain, the Seven Sisters (chalk cliffs along the southern coast), and the White Cliffs of Dover

Economy

Currency: Pound sterling

Population below poverty line: 17 % (of UK population)

Major natural resources: Limestone, chalk, coal, tin, oil, natural gas, iron ore, salt, gypsum, clay, lead, silica

Major agricultural products: Wheat and other cereal grains, potatoes, vegetables, seed oils, sheep, poultry, fish, dairy cows

Major exports: Chemicals, petroleum, medicines, foods, tobacco, beverages

Major imports: Machinery, automobiles, processed foods and beverages, footwear, clothing, chemicals

Historical Timeline

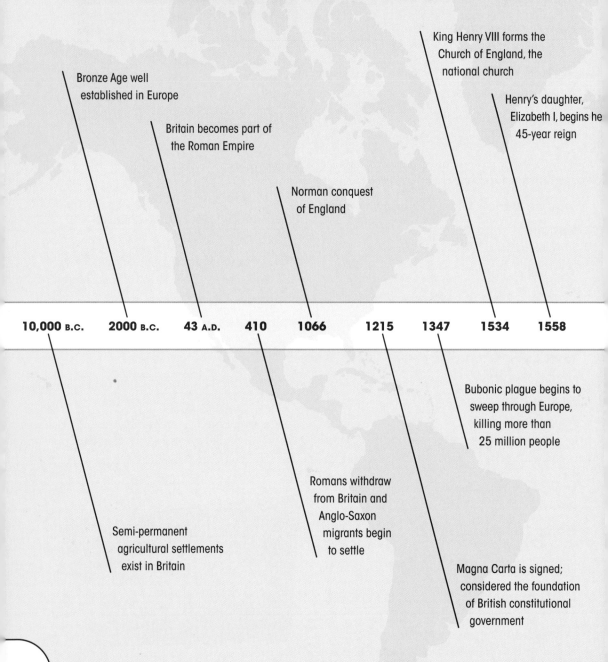

King Henry VIII forms the
Church of England, the
national church

Bronze Age well
established in Europe

Henry's daughter,
Elizabeth I, begins he
45-year reign

Britain becomes part of
the Roman Empire

Norman conquest
of England

| 10,000 B.C. | 2000 B.C. | 43 A.D. | 410 | 1066 | 1215 | 1347 | 1534 | 1558 |

Bubonic plague begins to
sweep through Europe,
killing more than
25 million people

Romans withdraw
from Britain and
Anglo-Saxon
migrants begin
to settle

Semi-permanent
agricultural settlements
exist in Britain

Magna Carta is signed;
considered the foundation
of British constitutional
government

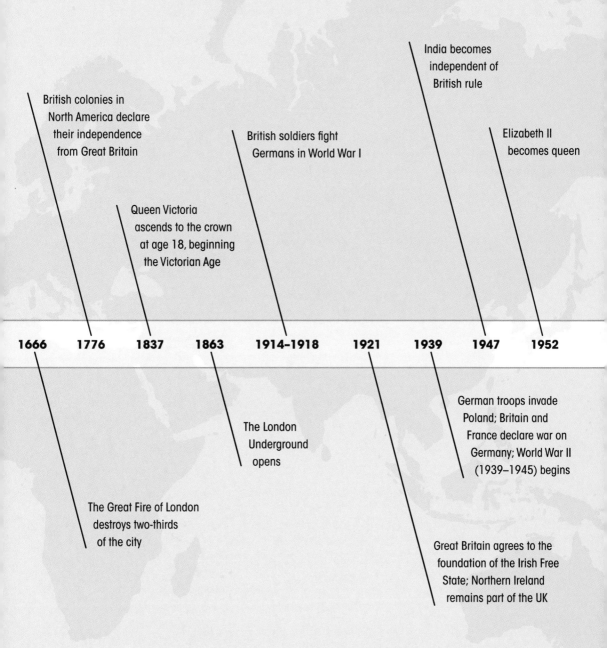

British colonies in
North America declare
their independence
from Great Britain

India becomes
independent of
British rule

British soldiers fight
Germans in World War I

Elizabeth II
becomes queen

Queen Victoria
ascends to the crown
at age 18, beginning
the Victorian Age

1666   1776   1837   1863   1914–1918   1921   1939   1947   1952

German troops invade
Poland; Britain and
France declare war on
Germany; World War II
(1939–1945) begins

The London
Underground
opens

The Great Fire of London
destroys two-thirds
of the city

Great Britain agrees to the
foundation of the Irish Free
State; Northern Ireland
remains part of the UK

Historical Timeline

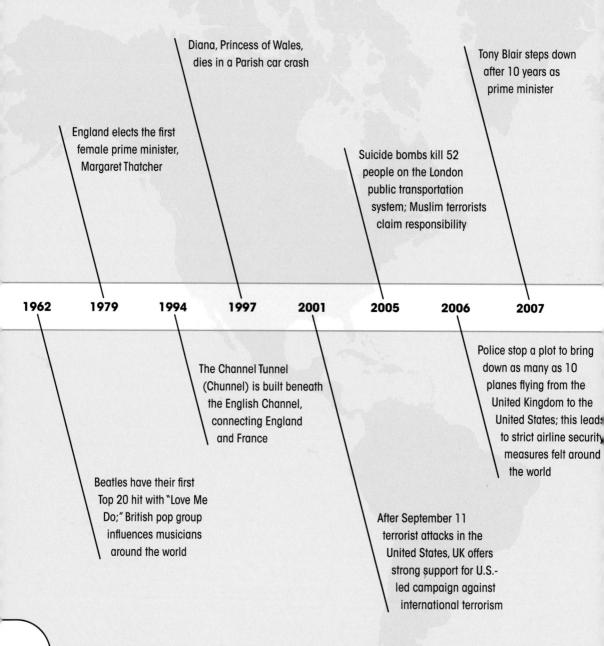

Diana, Princess of Wales, dies in a Parish car crash

Tony Blair steps down after 10 years as prime minister

England elects the first female prime minister, Margaret Thatcher

Suicide bombs kill 52 people on the London public transportation system; Muslim terrorists claim responsibility

| 1962 | 1979 | 1994 | 1997 | 2001 | 2005 | 2006 | 2007 |

Police stop a plot to bring down as many as 10 planes flying from the United Kingdom to the United States; this leads to strict airline security measures felt around the world

The Channel Tunnel (Chunnel) is built beneath the English Channel, connecting England and France

Beatles have their first Top 20 hit with "Love Me Do;" British pop group influences musicians around the world

After September 11 terrorist attacks in the United States, UK offers strong support for U.S.-led campaign against international terrorism

Glossary

alumni	the graduates of an educational institution
aptitude	a natural ability
assessment	a judgment of something's importance, size, or value
compulsory	required, often by law
diversity	the condition of being varied
effigy	a crude figure of a disliked person
evaluate	to judge or determine the value of something
government-sponsored	supported financially by funding from the government
gross domestic product	the total value of all goods and services produced in a country during a specific period
national curriculum	the courses of study that a nation requires schools to offer
nuclear family	the family group that consists of a father, mother, and children
persecution	cruel or unfair treatment, often because of race or religious beliefs
pounds	the monetary unit of the United Kingdom
technical school	a school that prepares students to enter a particular field of employment, usually a field that requires skilled workers, such as mechanics, plumbers, or carpenters
tuition	fee paid to attend a school

Additional Resources

IN THE LIBRARY

Fiction and nonfiction titles to further enhance your introduction to teens in England, past and present.

Cottrell Boyce, Frank. *Millions*. New York: Harper Collins, 2004.

Horowitz, Anthony. *The Devil and His Boy*. New York: Philomel, 2000.

Hussey, Charmian. *The Valley of Secrets*. New York: Simon & Schuster, 2006.

McKay, Hilary. *Caddy Ever After*. New York: Margaret K. McElderry Books, 2006.

Rabin, Staton. *Betsy and the Emperor*. New York: Simon Pulse, 2006.

Whelan, Gloria. *Listening for Lions*. New York: HarperCollins, 2005.

Hill, Barbara W. *Cooking the English Way*. Minneapolis: Lerner, 2002.

Toht, Betony. *Daily Life in Ancient and Modern London*. Minneapolis: Runestone Press, 2001.

ON THE WEB

For more information on this topic, use FactHound.

1. Go to www.facthound.com
2. Type in this book ID: 0756520614
3. Click on the Fetch It button.

Look for more Global Connections books.

Teens in Australia

Teens in Brazil

Teens in Canada

Teens in China

Teens in Egypt

Teens in France

Teens in India

Teens in Iran

Teens in Israel

Teens in Japan

Teens in Kenya

Teens in Mexico

Teens in Nigeria

Teens in Russia

Teens in Saudi Arabia

Teens in South Korea

Teens in Spain

Teens in Venezuela

Teens in Vietnam

Source Notes

Page 16, column 1, line 9: "Eton Today." Eton College. 7 March 2007. www.etoncollege.com/eton.asp?di=54

Page 40, column 2, line 18: United Kingdom. British Embassy in Washington, D.C. "Multicultural Britain." Britain USA. 7 March 2007. www.britainusa.com/sections/index_nt1.asp?i=41084

Page 51, column 1, line 14: Emma Ulrich. E-mail interview. 30 Jan. 2006.

Page 51, column 2, line 17: Rob Farrington. E-mail interview. 1 Feb. 2006.

Page 52, sidebar, column ?, line ?: Denis Campbell. "Plans for Clamp on Teenage Smoking." Guardian Unlimited. 22 April 2007. 11 May 2007. http://observer.guardian.co.uk/uk_news/story/0,,2062973,00.html

Page 58, column 2, line 17: Jay Gomez. E-mail interview. 31 Jan. 2006.

Page 58, column 2, line 37: Emma Ulrich.

Page 60, column 2, line 3: "Remember Remember the Fifth of November." Nursery Rhymes—Lyrics and Origins. 7 March 2007. www.rhymes.org.uk/remember remember the 5th november.htm

Page 60, column 2, line 10: Jay Gomez.

Pages 84–85, At a Glance: United Kingdom. National Statistics. www.statistics.gov.uk/default.asp; and United States. Central Intelligence Agency. *The World Factbook—United Kingdom*. 8 March 2007. 9 March 2007. www.cia.gov/library/publications/the-world-factbook/geos/uk.html

Select Bibliography

Alcohol Concern. *Young People's Drinking Fact Sheet: Summary.* November 2005. www.alcoholconcern.org.uk/servlets/doc/804

Conway, Edmund. "Revealed: The Real Rate of Inflation." *Telegraph.*12 May 2006. 10 April 2007. www.telegraph.co.uk/news/main.jhtml?xml=/news/2006/12/04/ ninflation04.xml

"Country Profile: United Kingdom." *BBC News*. 21 Feb. 2007. 10 April 2007. http:// news.bbc.co.uk/1/hi/world/europe/country_profiles/1038758.stm

"Drink Message 'Does Get Through.'" *BBC News*. 14 Sept. 2006. 9 Jan. 2007. http://news.bbc.co.uk/2/hi/uk_news/5345566.stm

Easton, Mark. "Why UK Teenagers Struggle to Cope." *BBC News*. 2 Nov. 2007. 9 March 2007. http://news.bbc.co.uk/2/hi/uk_news/6109916.stm

"Eton Today." Eton College. 7 March 2007. www.etoncollege.com/eton. asp?di=54

Farrington, Rob. E-mail interview. 1 Feb. 2006.

Gomez, Jay. E-mail interview. 31 Jan. 2006.

Lapidge, Michael, ed. *The Blackwell Encyclopedia of Anglo-Saxon England.* Malden, Mass.: Blackwell, 1999.

Morgan, Kenneth O., ed. *The Oxford Illustrated History of Britain.* New York: Oxford University Press, 1984.

Moxon, Irene. Personal interview. 1 Feb. 2006.

"Picking the Perfect Part Time Job." *TeenIssues*. 9 March 2007. www.teenissues.co.uk/PickingThePerfectTimeJob.html

"Remember Remember the Fifth of November." Nursery Rhymes— Lyrics and Origins. 7 March 2007. www.rhymes.org.uk/remember remember the 5th november.htm

Roberts, Bob. "The Bad Boys and Girls of Europe." *Mirror.co.uk* 3 Nov. 2006. 9 Jan. 2007. www.mirror.co.uk/news/tm_headline=the-bad-boys-and-girls-of-europe-&method=full&objecti d=18037434&siteid=94762-name_page.html

"The Schools System in England." *BBC Action Network*. 12 May 2006. 10 April 2007. www. bbc.co.uk/dna/actionnetwork/A1181792

Smith, Godfrey. *The English Companion: An Idiosyncratic Guide to England and Englishness.* New York: Viking Penguin, 1985.

Tan, Terry. *Culture Shock! Britain: Guide to Customs and Etiquette*. Portland, Ore.: Marshall Cavendish Editions, 2005.

Ulrich, Emma. E-mail interview. 30 Jan. 2006.

United Kingdom. British Embassy in Washington D.C. "The History of Multicultural Britain." Britain USA. 7 March 2007. www. britainusa.com/sections/articles_show_nt1. asp?d=11&i=281&L1=41013&L2=41084&L3= 41084&a=26006

United Kingdom. British Embassy in Washington D.C. "Multicultural Britain." Britain USA. 7 March 2007. www.britainusa.com/ sections/index_nt1.asp?i=41084

United Kingdom. Central Office of Inform-ation. Directgov. *Education and Learning.* 9 March 2007. www.direct.gov.uk/en/ EducationAndLearning/index.htm

United Kingdom. Central Office of Information. Directgov. *Planning a Career.* 9 March 2007. www.direct.gov.uk/en/YoungPeople/ Workandcareers/Planningyourfuture/DG_ 066169

United Kingdom. National Statistics. *Dependent Children.* 7 July 2005. 9 March 2007. www.statistics.gov.uk/CCI/nugget. asp?ID=1163&Pos=&ColRank=1&Rank=374

United Kingdom. National Statistics. *Families: Married Couple Families Still the Majority.* 7 July 2005. 9 March 2007, www.statistics.gov.uk/CCI/nugget. asp?ID=1161&Pos=2&ColRank=2&Rank=1000

United States. Central Intelligence Agency. *The World Factbook—United Kingdom.* 8 March 2007. 9 March 2007. www.cia.gov/library/ publications/the-world-factbook/geos/uk.html

United States. Department of State. Bureau of European and Eurasian Affairs. *Background Note: United Kingdom.* Washington, D.C., Feb. 2007. 10 April 2007. http://state.gov/r/pa/ ei/bgn/3846.htm

Watts, Michael. "England." *Teen Life in Europe.* Ed. Shirley R. Steinberg. Westport, Conn.: Greenwood Press, 2005.

Weisser, Henry G. *Understanding the U.K.* New York: Hippocrene Books, Inc., 1987.

Index

About the Author
Elizabeth Willingham

Elizabeth Willingham received a master's degree from Minnesota State University, Mankato. She has studied English literature, writing, and teaching English as a second or foreign language.

About the Content Adviser
Mark Bevir, Ph.D.

Political science professor Mark Bevir brought his personal interest and cultural expertise to his review of *Teens in England*. Dr. Bevir was born and raised in London and studied at the University of Oxford. Currently he teaches at the University of California, Berkeley, where he served as the acting director of the Center for British Studies. He is the author of several books and more than 100 scholarly articles.